W9-BWV-675

ANNIE ERNAUX

HAPPENING

Translated from the French by

TANYA LESLIE

SEVEN STORIES PRESS

New York / Oakland / London

Seven Stories Press
140 Watts Street
New York, NY 10013
www.sevenstories.com

Library of Congress Cataloging-in-Publication Data

Names: Ernaux, Annie, 1940 author. | Leslie, Tanya, translator.
Title: Happening / Annie Ernaux ; translated from the French by Tanya Leslie.
Other titles: Evâenement. English
Description: Second edition. | New York : Seven Stories Press, [2019]
Identifiers: LCCN 2019006834| ISBN 9781609809485 (paperback) | ISBN 9781609802264 (ebook)
Subjects: LCSH: Ernaux, Annie, 1940- | Authors, French--20th century--Biography. | Abortion--France. | BISAC: FICTION / Literary. | FICTION / Contemporary Women.
Classification: LCC PQ2665.R67 Z46413 2019 | DDC 843/.914 [B] --dc23
LC record available at https://lccn.loc.gov/2019006834

9 8 7 6 5 4 3 2

College professors and high school and middle school teachers may order free examination copies of Seven Stories Press titles. Visit https://www.sevenstories.com/pg/resources-academics or email academics@sevenstories.com.

Book design by Cindy LaBreacht

HAPPENING

I wish for two things:
that happening turn to writing.
And that writing be happening.

MICHEL LEIRIS

I wonder if memory is not simply a question
of following things through to the end.

YÛKO TSUSHIMA

I GOT OFF AT BARBÈS MÉTRO STATION. Like last time, men were idly waiting, clustered at the foot of the overhead subway. People were trudging along the sidewalk with pink shopping bags from the discount store Tati. I turned into the Boulevard Magenta and recognized the clothing store Billy with its anoraks hanging outside. A woman was walking toward me—plump legs sheathed in black stockings with a bold pattern. The Rue Amboise-Paré was almost empty until you reached the vicinity of the hospital. I made my way down the long passage inside the Elisa wing. For the first time I noticed a bandstand in the courtyard running along the glassed-in corridor. I wondered how I would be seeing all this on the way back. I walked through door 15 and up two floors to the reception area of the screening unit. I handed the secretary a card with my number. She consulted a box of files and pulled out a brown envelope containing documents. I held out my hand but she didn't give it to me. She laid it down on the desk, instructing me to take a seat and wait for my name to be called out.

The waiting room consists of two adjoining areas. I chose the one nearer the doctor's office, where there were more people. I began marking the essays I had brought with me. Soon afterward, a very young girl with long blonde hair handed over her card. I made sure that she too was not given an envelope and was told to sit down and wait. The people already waiting there were seated far apart: a man in his thirties, fashionably dressed with a receding hairline; a young black guy with a walkman; a middle-aged man with weathered features, slumped in his seat. After the fair-haired girl, a fourth man strode into the room: he settled confidently in a chair and pulled out a book from his briefcase. Then a couple arrived: the girl in leggings stretched over a pregnant stomach, the man in a business suit.

There were no magazines on the table, only a few leaflets on the nutritional value of dairy produce and "how to come to terms with AIDS." The woman in leggings was speaking to her companion; she kept standing up, embracing him, caressing him. He remained silent and motionless, both hands stiffly resting on an umbrella. The girl with sandy hair was staring at the floor, her eyes half-closed, a leather jacket folded over her knees; she seemed petrified. At her feet lay a large overnight bag and a small backpack. I wondered if she had any particular reason to be worried. Maybe she had come to pick up her results before going away for the weekend or visiting her parents in the country. The lady doctor emerged from her office—a young woman, slim, vivacious, in a coral skirt and black stockings. She called out a number. No one stood up. It was someone from the next room, a boy who hurried by; I glimpsed a pony tail and glasses.

The young black man was summoned, then someone from the other room. No one moved or spoke, except the woman in leggings. The only time we all looked up was when the lady doctor appeared in the doorway or when someone left her office. We would follow them with our eyes.

The telephone rang several times—people wanting an appointment or inquiring about opening hours. At one point, the receptionist left the room and came back with a biologist to answer a call. He kept saying, "no, your count is normal, perfectly normal." His words rang out ominously in the quiet room. The person on the phone was bound to be HIV positive.

I had finished marking my essays. I kept picturing the same blurred scene—one Saturday and Sunday in July, the motions of lovemaking, the ejaculation. This scene, buried for months, was the reason for my being here today. I likened the embracing and writhing of naked bodies to a dance of death. I felt that the man whom I had half-heartedly agreed to see again had come all the way from Italy with the sole purpose of giving me AIDS. Yet I couldn't associate the two: lovemaking, warm skin and sperm and my presence in the waiting room. I couldn't imagine sex ever being related to anything else.

The lady doctor called out my name. Before I had even entered her office, she flashed a broad grin at me. I took this to be a good sign. Closing the door, she immediately said, "the tests are negative." I burst out laughing. I paid no attention to what she said after that. She seemed in a happy, mischievous mood.

I rushed down the two flights of stairs and walked back the same way in a trance. I told myself that once again I had been saved. I wondered if the girl with long blonde hair had been saved too. At Barbès station, crowds stood facing each other across the platforms, with occasional bursts of pink Tati bags.

I realized that I had lived through these events at Lariboisière Hospital the same way I had awaited Dr. N's verdict in 1963, swept by the same feelings of horror and disbelief. So it would appear my life is confined to the period separating the Ogino method from the age of cheap condom dispensers. It's one way of measuring it, possibly the most reliable one of all.

IN OCTOBER 1963, IN THE CITY OF ROUEN, I waited for my period for over a week. It was a warm, sunny month. I felt heavy and stuffy in my winter coat, especially in the department stores where I had taken to browsing and buying stockings, waiting for college to resume. When I got back to my room in the girls' dorm in the Rue d'Herbouville, I would still hope to see a stain appear on my panties. I began writing in my diary every evening—the word NOTHING in big, underlined capital letters. I would wake up in the middle of the night and instinctively know that "nothing" had happened. The year before, around the same time, I had started work on a novel; now this seemed faraway, something that was not to be pursued.

One afternoon I went to see *Il Posto,* an Italian film in black and white. It was the slow, sad story of a young man working as an office clerk—his very first job. The cinema was almost empty. As I watched the frail figure of the boy in his cheap raincoat, the humiliations he suffered during his pathetic existence, somehow I knew the bleeding would not come back.

One evening I was talked into going to the theater by some of the girls who had gotten a spare ticket. They were putting on *Huis Clos* by Jean-Paul Sartre and I had never been to see a contemporary production. The theater was packed. I stared at the brightly lit stage at the back, obsessed with the fact that I no longer had my period. All I can remember about the play is the character called Estelle, a blonde girl in a blue dress, and the Boy dressed as a manservant, with red, lidless eyes. In my diary I wrote: "Fantastic. If only I didn't have this REALITY inside me."

By the end of October I had given up hope. I made an appointment to consult a gynecologist, Dr. N, on November 8.

On All Saints' Day I went back to spend the weekend with my parents as I did every year. I was afraid my mother would ask me why my period was late. I was sure she kept an eye on my underwear as she sorted through the dirty linen I would bring her once a month.

The following Monday I woke up feeling queasy, with a strange taste in my mouth. The druggist gave me a bottle of Hépatoum, a thick greenish liquid that made me feel worse.

O, one of the girls from the dorm, suggested that I fill in for her and teach French at a convent school, the Institution Saint-Dominique. It was a great opportunity to earn some money on top of my scholarship. I was received by Mother Superior. She was holding a copy of the sixteenth-century Lagarde et Michard.* I told her that I had never taught before and that the idea scared me. That was perfectly normal, she herself had been unable to enter a philosophy class for two years without keeping her head down and her eyes glued to the floor. Seated opposite me, she mimicked the scene. Suddenly all I could see was her veiled skull. As I was leaving with the Lagarde et Michard, I pictured myself in fifth form under the close scrutiny of the girls and I felt

---

* The standard textbook for French literature in schools throughout the country from the mid-Fifties to the Eighties.

quite sick. The next day I called Mother Superior and told her I had changed my mind. In a curt voice, she instructed me to return the book.

On Friday November 8, walking toward the Place de l'Hôtel-de-Ville to catch a bus to the Rue Lafayette where I had an appointment with Dr. N, I ran into Jacques S, a humanities student whose father ran a local factory. He asked me why I was heading for the Left Bank. I replied that I had a stomach ache and was going to see a stomatologist. He quickly put me right; a stomatologist is a specialist for mouth disorders, not stomach complaints. Fearing that he might suspect something because of my slip and might offer to accompany me to the doctor's office, I took leave of him hurriedly when the bus drew up.

As I clambered down from the examination table, my thick green sweater falling back onto my thighs, the gynecologist informed me that I was most certainly pregnant. What I had taken to be stomach pains were bouts of morning sickness. He prescribed injections to bring back the bleeding although he seemed to doubt their effectiveness. On the doorstep he beamed at me, "love children are the most beautiful of all." What a terrible statement.

I returned to my accommodation on foot. In my diary I wrote: "I am pregnant. It's a nightmare."

In early October, on several occasions I had made love with P, a political science student whom I had met during the summer vacation and whom I had been to see in Bordeaux. According to the Ogino method for birth control, I was in a risky period but somehow I couldn't imagine that it would "catch on" inside my loins. When I made love and climaxed, I felt that my body was basically no different from that of a man.

All the images I had of my stay in Bordeaux—the room giving onto the Cours Pasteur with its constant roar of traffic, the narrow bed, the sidewalk tables of the Café Montaigne, the cinema where we had been to see a historical epic, *The Rape of the Sabine Women*—had come to mean only one thing: I was there and I didn't know I was becoming pregnant.

The nurse on the university staff gave me an injection that evening, making no comment, and another one the following morning. It was the weekend of November 11, Armistice Day. I went back to stay with my parents. At one point, I had a brief discharge of a pink, watery liquid. I placed my soiled underwear and cotton pants on top of the pile of dirty linen, clearly in view. (In my diary: "A false alarm. Something to set my mother off the track.") Back in Rouen, I called Dr. N, who confirmed my condition and announced that he would send me a certificate. I received it the next day. Pregnancy certificate of: *Mademoiselle Annie Duchesne*. Date of delivery: *July 8, 1964*. I saw summer, sunshine. I tore up the certificate.

I wrote to P, informing him that I was pregnant and had no intention of keeping it. Neither of us had seemed particularly keen to pursue the relationship and it gave me pleasure to ruffle his carefree attitude. Naturally, I had no delusions about the fact that he would be greatly relieved on learning that I planned to abort.

One week later Kennedy was assassinated in Dallas. By then I had lost interest in that sort of thing.

The following months drifted by in a radiant state of limbo. I can see myself walking, wandering through the streets. Thinking back to this period, I am reminded of literary titles such as "the voyage out," "beyond good and evil" or "journey to the end of the night." I feel they are the perfect illustration of everything I lived through and experienced at the time—something indescribable and of great beauty.

For years these events have occupied my mind. Reading about an abortion in a novel immediately plunges me into a state of shock that shatters thoughts and images, as if words had metamorphosed into a maelstrom of emotions. Similarly, every time I chance upon a song that helped me cope during that period—*La Javanaise, J'ai la Mémoire qui Flanche*—I am deeply upset.

I began this story one week ago, not knowing whether I would go through with it. I just wanted to make sure that the urge to write was still there—the same urge that would seize me as soon as I sat down to the book that I embarked upon two years ago. Despite my efforts to fight it, I became obsessed with the idea. Obeying this impulse seemed a terrifying prospect. On the other hand, I could die tomorrow without having done anything about it. If I were guilty of anything, it would be that. One night I dreamed I was holding a book I had published about my abortion: it was unavailable from bookstores and didn't feature in any catalog. On the bottom of the cover, in huge letters, were the words: OUT OF PRINT. I couldn't decide whether the dream meant that I should write the book, or that there would be no point in doing so.

Through this story, time has been jerked into action and it is dragging me along with it. Now I know that I am determined to go through with this, whatever the cost, in the same way I was determined to go through with my abortion after tearing up the pregnancy certificate, aged 23.

I want to become immersed in that part of my life once again and learn what can be found there. This investigation must be seen in the context of a narrative, the only genre able to transcribe an event that was nothing but time flowing inside and outside of me. The diary and the engagement book I kept back then will provide the necessary dates and evidence to establish what happened. Above all I shall endeavor to revisit every single image until I feel that I have physically bonded with it, until a few words spring forth, of which I can say, "yes, that's it." I shall try to conjure up each of the sentences engraved in my memory which were either so unbearable or so comforting to me at the time that the mere thought of them today engulfs me in a wave of horror or sweetness.

The fact that my personal experience of abortion, i.e. clandestinity, is a thing of the past does not seem a good enough reason to dismiss it. Paradoxically, when a new law abolishing discrimination is passed, former victims tend to remain silent on the grounds that "now it's all over." So what went on is surrounded by the same veil of secrecy as before. Today abortion is no longer outlawed and this is precisely why I can afford to steer clear of the social views and inevitably stark formulas of the rebel Seventies—"abuse against women"—and face the reality of this *unforgettable* event.

(Leg. sp.)—The following persons shall be liable to both a fine and a term of imprisonment: 1) those responsible for performing abortive pratices; 2) those physicians, midwives, pharmacists and other individuals guilty of suggesting or encouraging such practices; 3) those women who have aborted at their own hands or at the hands of others; 4) those guilty of instigating abortion and spreading propaganda advocating contraception. The guilty parties may also receive an injunction requesting that they leave the country. Moreover, those belonging to the second category will be deprived of the right to exercise their profession either temporarily or definitively.

Nouveau Larousse Universel
1948 edition

TIME CEASED TO BE A SERIES of meaningless days punctuated by university talks and lectures, afternoons spent in cafés and at the library, leading up to exams and the summer vacation, to the future. It became a shapeless entity growing inside me which had to be destroyed at all costs.

I attended literature and sociology classes, I ate in the university canteen, I drank coffee twice a day at La Faluche, the students' hangout. Yet I was living in a different world. There were the other girls, with their empty bellies, and there was me.

To convey my predicament, I never resorted to descriptive terms or expressions such as "I'm expecting," "pregnant" or "pregnancy." They endorsed a future event that would never materialize. There was no point naming something that I was planning to get rid of. In my diary I would write, "it" or "that thing," only once "pregnant."

I would waver between sheer disbelief that it should have happened to me of all people, and the firm conviction that it was bound to happen to me. I'd had it coming to me since I had climaxed alone in bed, aged fourteen, and had frequently repeated the experience, despite prayers to the Holy Virgin and a string of other saints, entertaining fantasies that I was a whore. Indeed, it was truly a miracle that I hadn't found myself in this situation earlier. Until last summer, I had succeeded in not going all the way at the cost of considerable effort and humiliation, being branded either a slut or a cock teaser. Thankfully, I was saved by my impetuous feelings of lust which could find little gratification in flirting and which had therefore led me to fear even the most innocent kiss.

Somehow I felt there existed a connection between my social background and my present condition. Born into a family of laborers and storekeepers, I was the first to attend higher education and so had been spared both factory work and commerce. Yet neither my *baccalauréat* nor my B.A. in liberal arts had waived that inescapable fatality of the working-class—the legacy of poverty—embodied by both the pregnant girl and the alcoholic. My ass had caught up with me, and the thing growing inside me I saw as the stigma of social failure.

I wasn't the least bit apprehensive about getting an abortion. It seemed a highly feasible undertaking, admittedly not an easy one, but one that did not require undue courage. A minor ordeal. All I needed to do was follow in the footsteps of the myriad women who had preceded me. Since my early teens I had gleaned many stories of abortions, taken from novels or inspired by local gossip through hushed conversations. I had acquired some vague idea about which methods to use—a knitting needle, parsley stalks, injections of soapy water or violent horse rides—the ideal solution being to find a quack doctor or a back-street abortionist; both charged extremely high fees although I had no idea how much. The previous year, a young divorcee had told me that a doctor from Strasbourg had rid her of a child, sparing me the details except, "it was so painful I was clinging to the washbowl." I too was prepared to cling to the washbowl. Little did I know it could cost me my life.

Three days after tearing up the pregnancy certificate, as I was leaving the university buildings, I ran into Jean T, a married student with a steady job whom I had helped out two years earlier by sharing my notes of a lecture on Victor Hugo. His impassioned speech and revolutionary views appealed to me. We went and had a drink at the Café Métropole opposite the train station. At one point I hinted that I was pregnant, possibly because I thought he might offer to help me. I knew he belonged to a vaguely underground movement supporting free contraception and birth control and hoped his activities might prove useful.

His face instantly took on an intrigued, thrilled expression as though he could picture me with my legs wide apart, my vagina exposed. He may also have been amused by the sudden change from model student to desperate girl. He asked me who the father was and how long I'd been pregnant. He was the first person to whom I had mentioned my condition. Although he could offer no solution in the immediate future, the interest he showed was strangely comforting. He suggested we go back to his place for dinner, somewhere on the outskirts of Rouen. I didn't feel like going home to an empty room.

When we arrived, his wife was feeding their young child, seated in a highchair. Jean T said cursorily that I was in a spot of trouble. One of their friends turned up. After putting the child to bed, she served us rabbit stew with spinach. The green leaves glimpsed through the chunks of rabbit made me feel sick. I told myself that if I didn't get an abortion, by next year I would be just like his wife. After dinner she and the friend left to pick up some equipment for the grade school where she taught and I began washing the dishes with Jean T. He embraced me and said that we had enough time to make love. I pulled free and continued to wash the dishes. The child was crying in the room next to us, I felt like puking. Jean T kept pressing into me while he was drying the dishes. Then suddenly he resumed his normal tone of voice and pretended he was just testing my moral strength. His wife got back and they suggested that I stay the night. It was late and I imagine neither of them could face driving me back. I slept on an air bed in the drawing room. The next morning I was back in my room, complete with its student's gear, which I had left the day before, in the early afternoon. The bed was neatly made, nothing had been touched and almost a whole day had gone by. This is the sort of detail that tells us our life is beginning to fall apart.

I didn't think that Jean T had shown contempt for me. In his mind, I had moved on from the type of girl who might say no to the type who had undoubtedly said yes. At a time when this distinction was paramount and dictated boys' attitudes toward girls, Jean T was merely being pragmatic, confident that he could no longer get me pregnant since I was already expecting. It was an unpleasant episode but of very little consequence compared to my condition. He had promised to find me a doctor and I had no one else to turn to.

Two days later I dropped by his office and he took me out to lunch to a café on the quayside, near the bus station, in an unfamiliar area that had been bombed during the war and rebuilt in concrete. Recently I had began to wander, straying from my familiar surroundings and the places where I usually met up with other students. He ordered sandwiches. He was still fascinated by my condition. Laughing, he said that he and the boys could fit me with a probe. I wondered if he really meant it. Then he told me about the Bs, a married couple he knew; the wife had had an abortion a few years before, "mind you, she almost croaked in the process." He didn't know their address but I could get in touch with LB through the newspaper where she worked as a freelance journalist. I knew her by sight because we had both attended the same philology lecture—a small, dark girl with large spectacles and a stern appearance. After presenting her paper, she had been warmly congratulated by the professor. The fact that someone like her had gotten an abortion was a comfort to me.

When he had finished his sandwiches, Jean T settled back in his chair and beamed at me, exposing his widely spaced teeth, "God, do I love eating." I felt sick and lonely. I was beginning to realize that he wasn't too keen to get involved. Girls who chose to abort didn't quite embody the moral principles of his family planning association. What he wanted was to remain at the forefront and to find out how my story would end. It was a bit like seeing the show without having to pay the price. He had warned me that his involvement in a group campaigning in favor of planned pregnancy prevented him from lending me money for an illegal abortion "on moral grounds." (In my diary: "Had lunch with T along the banks. More problems.")

My quest had started. It was imperative that I track down LB. At one time I used to see her husband handing out tracts at the university canteen but apparently he had stopped coming. I took to scouring lecture halls at noon and in the evening, hanging out in the lobby, keeping an eye on the door.

Two evenings in a row I waited for LB outside the editorial offices of *Paris-Normandie*. I dared not go inside and ask whether she had already arrived. I was afraid my behavior might come across as suspicious and the last thing I wanted was to hassle LB at her workplace for something that had almost done her in. On the second evening it was raining; I stood alone in the street, under my umbrella, scanning the newspaper pages pinned up on the wall, on a board protected by wire meshing, checking out both ends of the Rue de l'Hôpital. LB was someplace in Rouen; she was the only woman who could save me and she was nowhere to be found. Back in my room, I wrote: "Waited for LB in the rain once again. No luck. I'm getting desperate. This thing has got to go."

I had no clues, no lead.

Although abortion was mentioned in many novels, no details were given about what actually took place. There was a sort of void between the moment the girl learns she is pregnant and the moment it's all over. I looked up the word "abortion" in the library index. The only references I could find were to medical publications. I chose two—*Surgical and Medical Records* and *The Journal of Immunology*. I was hoping for practical information but the articles focused on the clinical consequences of "criminal abortion," which held no interest for me.

(I had jotted down the names and references of these magazines—*Per m 484, no 5, no 6, Norm. Mm 1065*—on the first page of my address book. These marks scribbled in blue ballpoint exert a strange fascination over me. Because of their physical, imperishable nature, these material traces may be more apt to convey reality than the subjective approach provided by memory or writing.)

One afternoon I set off, determined to find a doctor who would consent to perform an abortion. Surely that person could be found somewhere. Rouen had become a forest of gray stones. I peered at the brass plaques, wondering who lay behind each name. I couldn't make up my mind to ring the bell. I was waiting for a sign.

I began heading toward Martainville, a rough, working-class area where I imagined doctors might be more understanding.

A wan November sun shone over the city. As I walked, I began humming a tune that was often played on the radio—*Dominique, nique, nique*—performed by Soeur Sourire, a Dominican nun who also strummed the guitar. The lyrics were edifying and somewhat naive (Soeur Sourire didn't know the meaning of *niquer*) but the melody was gay and lively. Somehow it gave me the heart to go on. I turned into the Place St-Marc with its piles of empty market stalls. At the back stood the Froger furniture store where my mother and I had come to buy a wardrobe when I was a little girl. By now I had stopped noticing the plaques on doors; I was wandering around aimlessly.

(About ten years ago I read in the newspaper *Le Monde* that the Singing Nun, as she was known throughout the world, had committed suicide. The article stated that after the hugely successful hit *Dominique*, she had come into conflict with the clergy, had eventually left the orders and moved in with a woman. Over the years she had given up singing and had sunk into oblivion. She had taken to drinking. I was deeply moved by her story. She couldn't have imagined ever ending up that way—social misfit, alcoholic, renegade sister with homosexual proclivities. Yet this, I felt, was the woman who had held my hand as I roamed the streets of Martainville, a lost, solitary figure. We had both lost our bearings, although at different moments in time. What gave me the courage to go on living that afternoon was the voice of a woman who was to hit rock bottom and die. I passionately hoped that life had brought her some small glimmer of happiness and that, on those lonely, whisky-sodden evenings, having learned the contemporary meaning of *niquer*—to screw—she could tell herself that, at the end of the day, she really did screw all the other nuns.

Sœur Sourire is one of the many women I have never met, and with whom I might have very little in common, but who have always been close to my heart. Be they dead or alive, real people or fictional characters, they form an invisible chain of artists, authoresses, literary heroines and figures from my childhood. I feel that they embrace my own story.)

Like many doctor's offices in the Sixties, the one belonging to the GP on the Boulevard de l'Yser, near the Place Beauvoisine, resembled a middle-class living room with its rugs, glassed-in bookcase and antique writing desk. I have no idea how I ended up in this residential quarter, home to André Marie, a right-wing member of the French Parliament. Night had fallen and it seemed a pity to go back without having tried my luck. An elderly doctor greeted me. I told him that I was feeling tired and that my period was late. After examining me with a two-finger stall, he informed me that I was most certainly pregnant. I hadn't the courage to ask him to perform the abortion, I simply begged him to make the bleeding come back, at any cost. He made no comment. Averting his glance, he then launched into a long diatribe against men who seduced young girls and then abandoned them. He wrote out a prescription for calcium capsules and injections of oestradiol. Toward the end of the visit, on learning that I was a student, he softened up and asked me if I knew Philippe D, the son of one of his friends. As it happened, I did know him—a dark, spectacled boy with an unprepossessing appearance who had attended Latin classes with me in freshman year and who had since left for Caen. I remember thinking that he was hardly the type to get me pregnant. "He's a real nice kid, huh?" The doctor was smiling; he was obviously pleased that I agreed. He seemed to have forgotten why I was there. He looked relieved as he walked me back to the front door. He didn't tell me to come back.

Girls like me were a waste of time for doctors. With no money and no connections—otherwise we wouldn't accidentally end up on their doorstep—we were a constant reminder of the law that could send them to jail and close down their practice for good. They would never tell us the truth, that they weren't prepared to sacrifice their career for some sweet chick foolish enough to get knocked up. Or maybe their sense of duty was such that they would have chosen to die rather than break a law that could cost women their lives. They must have assumed that most women would go through with the abortion anyway in spite of the ban. All in all, plunging a knitting needle into a womb weighed little next to ruining one's career.

It has cost me quite some effort to resist the powerful hold of these images and leave behind the pale winter sunshine flooding the Place Saint-Marc in Rouen, the lyrics of Soeur Sourire or even the hushed atmosphere of the medical office on the Boulevard de l'Yser, belonging to a physician whose name I have long forgotten. To capture that invisible, elusive reality unknown to memory that had sent me scouring the streets in search of an unlikely doctor—the law.

The law was everywhere. In the euphemisms and understatements of my diary; the bulging eyes of Jean T; the so-called forced marriages, the musical *The Umbrellas of Cherbourg*, the shame of women who aborted and the disapproval of those who did not. In the sheer impossibility of ever imagining that one day women might be able to abort freely. As was often the case, you couldn't tell whether abortion was banned because it was wrong or wrong because it was banned. People judged according to the law, they didn't judge the law.

I doubted that the injections prescribed by the doctor would have any effect but I was willing to try anything. Fearing that the nurse from college might be suspicious, I decided to ask a medical student whom I had often seen at the canteen. That evening she sent a colleague of hers round to my room, a pretty blonde girl, perfectly at ease. On seeing her, I realized how low I was slipping. She gave me the injection without asking any questions. The following day, since neither of the girls was available, I sat down on the bed, screwed up my eyes and plunged the needle into my thigh. (The entry in my diary read: "Two injections and still nothing.") Later on, I learned that the drug prescribed by the doctor on the Boulevard de l'Yser was used to prevent women from miscarrying.

(I feel that this narrative is dragging me along in a direction I have not chosen, proceeding along the inescapable road of fatality. I must resist the urge to rush through these days and weeks, and attempt to convey the unbearable sluggishness of that period as well as the feeling of numbness that characterizes dreams, resorting to all the means at my disposal—attention to detail, use of a descriptive past tense, analysis of events.)

I PURSUED MY NORMAL ROUTINE—attending classes and working at the library. That summer, in a burst of enthusiasm, I had chosen women in Surrealist writing as the subject of my thesis. Now this topic seemed barely more exciting than the study of conjunctions in medieval French or the use of metaphors in Chateaubriand's work. I stared blankly at texts by Paul Éluard, André Breton and Louis Aragon that celebrated spiritual women forming a bond between mankind and the universe. Every now and then I would jot down a few sentences in connection with my thesis. Yet I couldn't put my notes in order and was quite incapable of meeting my tutor's request, which was to hand in the synopsis and first chapter of my work. Connecting different spheres of knowledge and incorporating them into a structured piece of writing was beyond my strength.

Since high school I had shown a certain talent for juggling with abstract concepts. Although I realized that dissertations and other such college assignments were purely academic, I was proud to excel in this field; I assumed this was the price to pay to "live among books," as my parents would say, and to devote my future existence to them.

Now these "intellectual heavens" were out of reach: I was wallowing down below, my body overcome by nausea. One moment I would be longing to regain my powers of reasoning once I had gotten rid of my problem. The next moment I believed that the knowledge I had acquired was but an artificial structure that had definitely collapsed. In a strange way, my inability to write my thesis was far more alarming than my need to abort. It was the unmistakable sign of my silent downfall. (My diary read: "I can't write. I can't work. Is there any way out of this mess?") I had stopped being "an intellectual." I don't know whether this feeling is widespread. It causes indescribable pain.

(I'm sure I could be more thorough in my analysis of things but I seem to be held back by something from my distant past, associated with the working-class world to which I belong, instinctively wary of "brain-racking," or with my own body, the remembrance of these events inside my body.)

Every morning, on waking up, I imagined the feeling of nausea had gone but seconds later it would well up inside me like a dark, sinister wave. I was seized with both desire and disgust for food. One day, walking past a butcher's, I spotted some salami in the window. I immediately went in, bought some and wolfed it down on the sidewalk. On another occasion, I begged some boy to buy me a glass of grape juice; I was so desperate I would have done anything to get my way. The sight of some foods made me feel sick; others, with a pleasing appearance, seemed to rot in my mouth.

One morning, while I was standing in the hall waiting for a lecture to end, the figures of the students around me suddenly broke up into small shiny dots. I barely had time to collapse onto the stairs.

In my diary I wrote: "Continual bouts of dizziness."—"I felt like puking at the library around 11."—"I am still sick."

During my first year at college I would fantasize about some of the boys without their knowing: I would stalk them, settling a few rows behind them in lecture halls, checking out when they came to the canteen or the library. These imaginary romances seemed a thing of the past—those were carefree days verging on childhood.

A photograph taken in September that year shows me sitting with my hair falling around my shoulders, a scarf knotted in the neckline of a striped blouse, sun-tanned, smiling, *mischievous*. Every time I look at it, I feel it was the very last picture of me as a young girl, caught up in the invisible yet pervasive web of seductiveness.

Out partying at La Faluche with a few other girls from the dorm, I felt attracted to the gentle, fair-haired boy with whom I had been dancing for most of the evening. The first time since I learned I was pregnant. So, nothing could stop a woman's cunt from stretching and opening, even when her belly already contained an embryo that would receive a stranger's spurt of semen without flinching. The entry in my diary read, "Danced with a romantic guy but *found it impossible* to go any further."

Everything people said seemed either naive or trivial. The habit some girls had of recounting the minutiae of their daily lives filled me with horror. One morning a student from Montpellier with whom I had attended philology classes sat down beside me in the library. She embarked on a detailed description of her new accommodation in the Rue Saint-Maur, her landlady, the linen drying in the hallway, her teaching job at a private school in the Rue Beauvoisine and so on. This meticulous, self-complacent account of her existence was both uncanny and obscene. I believe I can still recall everything she told me that day, in her Mediterranean accent, precisely because it was all so meaningless, and terrifying too since it signified my exclusion from the real world.

(Since I started writing about my abortion, I have been trying to conjure up the faces and names of the students I knew, most of whom I was never to see again after my move to Rouen the following year. Salvaged one by one from oblivion, they naturally resume their place in the life I had at the time, reappearing in college, at the local library, the university canteen or La Faluche, and on the station platform where they would flock on Friday evenings, waiting for a train to take them back home. A human crowd is gradually coming to life and I am caught up in it. This throng can revive the twenty-three-year-old that I was far more effectively than personal memories; it also reflects how deeply involved I was in the student community. These names and faces explain why I was so distressed: compared to such people embodying normality, I had become an emotional outcast.

I have no right to mention their names because I am not dealing with fictional characters but real people. Yet I find it hard to believe they are living somewhere out there. In a way, I am right: what makes up their life today—their physical appearance, their opinions, their bank accounts—bears no resemblance to the life they led back in the Sixties, the one I can see as I write. As soon as I feel like looking up their names in the electronic phone book, I realize this would be a mistake.)

I continued to visit my parents on weekends. Concealing my condition was no big deal: this was the type of relationship I'd had with them since adolescence. My mother belonged to the pre-war generation, marked by sin and shameful sex. I was certain that her beliefs were inviolable and my capacity to endure them rivalled only by her conviction that I shared such principles. Like most parents, mine imagined they could unfailingly detect the slightest sign of misconduct at a mere glance. All it took to set their minds at rest was to go on visiting them at regular intervals, sporting a broad smile and serene features, arriving with a bundle of dirty linen and leaving with a sack of provisions.

One Monday I came back from their place with a pair of knitting needles which I had bought one summer with the intention of making myself a cardigan. Two long, shiny blue needles. I had found no solution. I had decided to take the matter into my own hands.

On the previous evening I had been to see *Mein Kampf* * with a bunch of girls from the dorm. I was extremely agitated and kept thinking about what I planned to do the next day. The movie, however, did point to one blatant fact: the pain I was about to inflict on myself would be nothing compared to the suffering experienced in death camps. This thought gave me courage and heightened my determination. Also, knowing that hundreds of other women had been through the same thing was a comfort to me.

---

* A Swedish documentary about Nazi Germany made in 1961.

The following morning I lay down on my bed and slowly inserted a knitting needle into my vagina. I groped around, vainly trying to locate the opening of the womb; I stopped as soon as I felt pain. I realized I wasn't going to manage on my own. I was enraged by my own helplessness. I just wasn't up to it. "No luck. Impossible, damn it. I can't stop crying and I've just about had it."

(I realize this account may exasperate or repel some readers; it may also be branded as distasteful. I believe that any experience, whatever its nature, has the inalienable right to be chronicled. There is no such thing as a lesser truth. Moreover, if I failed to go through with this undertaking, I would be guilty of silencing the lives of women and condoning a world governed by male supremacy.)

After my unsuccessful attempt, I decided to call Doctor N. I told him that I didn't want to "keep it" and added that I had harmed myself in the process. It was a lie but I wanted to make quite clear I would stop at nothing to abort. He told me to come straight to his office. At that point, I still believed he might help me. He greeted me in silence, his face solemn. After examining me, he announced that all was well. I began weeping. He remained seated behind his desk, motionless, his head bowed, visibly upset. I thought he was still struggling against his conscience and was about to give in. Then he looked up: "Don't tell me where you're going, I don't want to know. Just make sure you take penicillin eight days before and after the operation. I'll write you out a prescription."

Leaving his office, I blamed myself for having ruined my last chance. Circumventing the law involved a number of stratagems and I had overestimated my powers of persuasion. More tears, more begging and a more realistic description of my predicament would undoubtedly have done the trick. (This I believed for many years. But I may have been wrong. Only he could say.) At least he was anxious that I should not die of blood poisoning.

Neither of us had mentioned the word abortion, not even once. This thing had no place in language.

(Last night I dreamed that I was back in 1963, desperately trying to get an abortion. When I woke up, I realized the dream had plunged me into the same state of despondency and helplessness I had experienced at the time. Then it struck me that the book I was writing was a doomed enterprise. I saw an analogy with orgasm, that split-second when we get to the "heart of things:" what I was trying to convey through writing had been achieved spontaneously and without any effort—making my literary venture a lost cause.

But now that impression has gone, the urge to write is all the more pressing since it has been justified by my dream.)

Among the students I knew, the only two girls whom I considered to be friends had both left. One had been sent away to the sanatorium in Saint-Hilaire-du-Touvet, the other was training to become a child psychologist in Paris. I had written to both of them, telling them I was pregnant and was seeking an abortion. Although neither criticized me, they seemed alarmed by the situation. Other people's fear was the last thing I needed; they could do nothing for me.

I had met O during my first year at college; her room was on the same floor as mine and we often went out together but I hardly thought of her as a friend. Girls invariably bitch about one another without this ever affecting or damaging their relationship and the prevailing opinion about O, which I shared, was that she was a nagging little bore. I knew she was greedy for secrets which she treasured and then bestowed on her peers, making herself worthy of interest for a couple of hours. Moreover, because of her bourgeois, Catholic upbringing and her observance of the Pope's teachings on contraception, she was probably the last person I should have turned to. Yet it was her I chose as my confidante that month of December, right up to the end. I realize now: I had to reveal my condition, regardless of people's beliefs or possible disapproval. Because I was so powerless, the act of telling them was crucial, its consequences immaterial: I simply needed to confront these people with the stark vision of reality.

Neither was I a close friend of André X, a freshman in the French department who delighted in recounting horrific tales taken from the satirical journal *Hara-Kiri*, delivering the details in a cold, detached voice. One day, while we were having a drink in a café, I let on that I was pregnant and would do anything to get an abortion. He sat there mesmerized, staring at me with big brown eyes. Then he tried to persuade me to follow the "natural way" and to refrain from committing what he regarded as a criminal act. We stayed there for a long time, huddled over a table in the Café Métropole, near the entrance. He couldn't bring himself to leave. I felt that his determination to make me change my mind was underpinned by a powerful emotion combining fear and fascination. Men found my desire to abort strangely enticing. I realized that for O, André and Jean T, my abortion was a story whose ending was unknown.

(It seems rather pointless to write, I can picture the Café Métropole, the small table where we were sitting, just by the door giving onto the Rue Verte, the inscrutable waiter called Jules who reminded me of the character in Sartre's *Being and Nothingness*, who liked to pass for a waiter, and so on. After all, imagining and remembering are the very essence of writing. Here, however, it's different: "I can picture" helps to convey that precise moment when I feel I have bonded with my former life, the one that has gone for ever, a feeling admirably rendered by the expression, "it feels like only yesterday.")

The only person who failed to show an interest was the boy who had gotten me pregnant, sending me infrequent letters from Bordeaux in which he alluded to the many problems that stood in the way of a solution. (My diary read: "He's leaving me to cope on my own.") I should have realized this meant he no longer cared and was anxious to resume his breezy lifestyle, concerned solely for his exams and future career. Instinctively I may have sensed this but I hadn't the courage to break up and compound my frantic search for an abortionist with the loneliness resulting from separation. This refusal to face reality was a *conscious* decision. Although I couldn't stand the sight of boys joking and guffawing in cafés—he was bound to be doing the same back in Bordeaux—it gave me an incentive to carry on disrupting his peaceful routine. In October we had arranged to spend our Christmas vacation at a winter resort with a young couple we knew. I had no intention of changing my plans.

We were approaching mid-December.

My buttocks and breasts strained against the dresses I wore and my body felt heavy, but the bouts of nausea had stopped. At times I would actually forget that I was two months' pregnant. Maybe it was because of this numbing process, in which our mind chooses to blot out the anxiety of D-day, that many girls would let weeks, then months go by, until they eventually gave birth. Lying on my bed, with the winter sunlight streaming through the window, I listened to the Brandenburg Concerti just like the year before. I felt that nothing in my life had changed.

In my diary, I wrote: "I feel that my pregnancy is totally abstract"—"I touch my belly, I know it's there. But that's as far as my imagination will go. If I let time have its way, by next July they'll be pulling a child out of me. But I can't feel it at all."

A week or so before Christmas, when I had more or less given up hope, LB came knocking at my door. Jean T had ran into her in town and had told her I needed to see her. She still had on her large, daunting spectacles with their black frames. She kept smiling at me. We sat down on my bed. She gave me the address of the woman with whom she had dealt, a middle-aged paramedic who worked at a clinic—Madame P-R, Impasse Cardinet, in the 17th *arrondissement* in Paris. I must have laughed on hearing the word *"impasse,"* which epitomized the sordid figure of the backstreet abortionist in popular literature, for she added that the Impasse Cardinet gave onto the Rue Cardinet, a main street. I didn't know Paris that well so the name meant nothing to me; all it suggested was a jewelry store, the Comptoir Cardinet, which was advertized daily on the radio. In a calm but cheerful voice, LB proceeded to tell me how Madame P-R worked: she inserted a probe into the opening of the womb using a speculum and all you had to do was wait until you miscarried. A reliable woman with high standards of hygiene, who sterilized all her tools. Such precautions, however, did not kill all the germs since LB had contracted septicemia. I could avoid that by asking a GP to prescribe antibiotics soon afterward for some minor ailment. I told her I already had a prescription for penicillin. It all seemed so easy and straightforward—after all, LB had lived through it and there she was, sitting right next to me. Mme P-R charged four hundred francs for her services. LB volunteered to lend me the money. An address and a few bank notes were the only things I needed right then.

(I must resort to initials when mentioning her name: she was the first in a series of women who lent me their support and whose knowledge, practical experience and wise decisions helped me to overcome this ordeal *as best I could.* I long to disclose her identity and reveal her lovely Christian name, symbolically chosen by exiled parents who had fled Franco's Spain. But the reason for my wanting to do this—the fact that she really does exist and deserves to be commended for her behavior— is precisely the reason that stops me from doing so. I have no right to expose a real, living woman like LB—I have just checked in the phone book—using a public medium such as a book, exercising a right which is not reciprocated: after all, she could quite rightly claim that she "didn't ask me for anything."

Last Sunday I made a detour via Rouen on my way back from the Normandy coast. I walked down the Rue du Gros-Horloge until I reached the cathedral. I settled at a café terrace in the Espace du Palais, a new shopping mall. The book I am writing has plunged me into the heart of the Sixties yet nothing in the colored, refurbished town center suggested that period. Only after considerable effort was I able to recapture the town back in those days, stripping it of its bright façades, reinstating its gray, drab appearance, reviving traffic in the pedestrian streets.

I stared at passers-by. I thought of that game where you have to make out silhouettes concealed among the lines of a drawing. Somewhere in the crowd there might be one of the students I had known in 1963: I can see them so clearly when I write, yet today they have become invisible to me. At a table nearby sat a handsome girl— chestnut hair, dark complexion, small, pouting lips—who reminded me of LB. I fondly imagined that she might be her daughter.)

Traveling to the Massif Central, meeting up with P, whose desire to see me again I seriously doubted, and spending part of the precious money I needed for the abortion was not a wise course of action. But I had never been to the mountains and I needed a few weeks' grace before facing the Impasse Cardinet, in the 17th *arrondissement*.

I gaze at a town plan of Le Mont-Dore in the Michelin guide and read the names of streets—Rue Meynadier, Rue Sidoine-Apollinaire, Rue Montlozier, Rue du Capitaine-Chazotte, Place du Panthéon and so on. I learn that the city features a spa and is cut across by the River Dordogne. I might just as well never have set foot there.

The entries in my diary read: "Danced at the Casino."—"Meeting up at La Tannerie."—"Went to La Grange last night." But all I can see is snow, and the crowded café where we would settle in the late afternoon with the jukebox playing *If I Had a Hammer*.

I remember the arguments, leading to tears and sulks, not the words. I cannot say what P meant to me at the time or what I expected from him. Probably the admission that my abortion was a sacrifice verging on an "act of love," despite my having made the decision purely in my own interest.

Annick and Gontran, the two law students accompanying us, were not aware that I was pregnant and wanted to abort. P had not deemed it necessary to inform them of the situation, dismissing them as bourgeois and conformist— they were engaged but did not sleep together. Above all, he seemed anxious not to spoil our vacation by bringing up this unfortunate business. His face would darken as soon as I mentioned the subject. Apparently, he had found no solution in Bordeaux. I very much doubted he had even tried.

The other couple, who were well-off, were staying in an expensive, old-fashioned hotel; P and I had checked into a modest inn. We made love hurriedly and infrequently, failing to take advantage of my predicament—after all, the harm was done—in the same way the unemployed seldom enjoy their new lease of life and freedom and the terminally ill carry on eating and drinking with customary moderation.

When the four of us were together, the prevailing mood was one of light-hearted banter, threatened briefly by some minor incident or caustic remark, soon forgotten in our quest for consensus. They had all worked hard at their subjects and had duly handed in their assignments; the carefree attitude they chose to flaunt was part of their reward for being good students. They wanted to have fun, to go dancing and to see movies like *Les Tontons Flingueurs*. My primary concern during that term had been to find a solution to my abortion. I tried hard to share their enthusiasm but somehow I wasn't up to it. I was the sort of girl who went with the flow.

I turned all my attention to sport, hoping that my strenuous efforts or maybe even a fall might dislodge "that thing," making it unnecessary for me to visit the woman in the 17th *arrondissement*. When Annick lent me her skiing gear, which I couldn't afford to hire, I would repeatedly tumble, imagining each time I did that I was inflicting the fall that would save me. One day, after P and Annick had refused to climb any further, accompanied by Gontran alone I decided to brave the summit of Puy Jumel in my fake leather boots with their flared tops that let in the snow. I trudged on ahead, my eyes glued to the slope, dazzled by the reflection, finding it more and more difficult to extricate my feet from the powdery snow, driven by the overriding urge to make that embryo let go. I was convinced I had to push back my own limits and reach the top of the mountain to get rid of it. I wore myself out to kill it under me.

Whenever I think about that week's vacation in Le Mont-Dore, I picture a shimmering stretch of snow and sunshine reaching into the dark recesses of January. No doubt because our primitive memory chooses to portray the past as a basic juxtaposition of light and shade, day and night.

(Writing invariably raises the issue of proof: apart from my engagement book and my diary, I have no sure indication of what I thought and felt back then because of the abstract, evanescent nature of what goes through our mind.

The only concrete evidence I have stems from the lingering sensations associated with people and things outside of me—the sparkling snow at Le Mont-Dore, Jean T's bulging eyes, the ballad of Soeur Sourire. True memory has to be material.)

On December 31 I left Le Mont-Dore with a family who had offered to give me a lift back to Paris. I didn't join in the conversation. At one point the woman said that the girl in the maid's room had miscarried, "she was moaning all night." All I remember about the journey was the rainy weather and that remark. This, and other sentences, either frightening or comforting, mostly from strangers, guided me toward the ordeal, supporting me like a viaticum until I too went through with it.

(I think I began this story because I wanted to follow the path leading up to those images of January '64, in the 17th *arrondissement.* Similarly, when I was fifteen, my whole life hinged on one or two images of me in the future: making love, traveling to faraway countries. I have no idea which words will come to me. I have no idea where my writing will take me. I would like to stall this moment and remain in a state of expectancy. Maybe I'm afraid that the act of writing will shatter this vision, just like sexual fantasies fade as soon as we have climaxed.)

On Wednesday January 8* I went up to Paris to meet the woman and settle practical details such as the date and her fees. To save buying a train ticket, I hitched a lift at the bottom of the Côte Sainte-Catherine, the main road leading out of town. In my state, taking extra risks seemed of little consequence. Sleet was falling. A large car pulled up, "a Jaguar" the driver replied when questioned. He drove in silence, holding the wheel at arm's length, with gloved hands. He dropped me at Neuilly and I took the Métro.

---

* For me, mentioning the date is an absolute necessity that reflects the reality of an event. It is the date that separates life from death for every one of us— November 22, 1963, in the case of John Fitzgerald Kennedy.

When I emerged into the 17th *arrondissement,* it was already dark. The street sign said "Passage Cardinet" and not "Impasse Cardinet"—an encouraging sign. I reached number…, an old, dilapidated building. Madame P-R lived on the third floor.

Thousands of girls have climbed up stairs and knocked on a door answered by a woman who is a complete stranger, to whom they are about to entrust their stomach and their womb. And that woman, the only person who can rid them of their misfortune, would open the door, in an apron and patterned slippers, clutching a dish towel, and inquire, "Yes, Miss, can I help you?"

Madame P-R was a short, plump woman with spectacles, dark clothes and gray hair worn in a bun. She looked like an elderly peasant. She quickly ushered me into a dark, narrow kitchen leading to a slightly larger area with old-fashioned furniture—the only two rooms in the flat. She asked me when I'd had my last period. According to her, three months was just about the right time to do it. She made me unbutton my coat and felt my stomach with both hands over my skirt, exclaiming excitedly, "my, that's some belly you've got!" When I mentioned my exertions in the snow, she shrugged her shoulders and snapped, "what do you expect, the mountain air will have done it good!" She spoke of it gleefully as of an evil creature.

I was standing by the bed, facing a woman with a sullen complexion, who spoke fast, with quick, jumpy movements. This was the woman to whom I would surrender my insides, this was where it would all happen.

She told me to come back the following Wednesday, the only day of the week when she could bring back a vaginal speculum from the hospital where she worked. She would insert the probe on its own—no soapy water, no bleach. She confirmed her fees, four hundred francs, to be paid in cash. She attended to her business with quiet determination. Without being overfamiliar—she didn't address me as "*tu*"—or inquisitive—she asked no questions—she focused on the essentials of the job: the date of my last period, the price, the technique used. This emphasis on practicality was strangely comforting. No feelings, no morals. By experience Madame P-R knew that a conversation confined to basics avoided the tears and emotional outbursts that might lead the girls to procrastinate or even change their minds.

Later on, when I recalled her blinking eyes, her habit of chewing on her lower lip and that slightly haunted expression, it occurred to me that she too might have been afraid. Nothing, however, would have stopped her from doing what she did, just like nothing would have stopped me from having the abortion. Clearly, money was a strong motive but she may also have felt she was helping women. Moreover, for someone who spent all day emptying the basins of the sick and pregnant, enjoying the same authority as doctors who barely noticed her, practicing in a two-room apartment in the Passage Cardinet must have given her a secret thrill. Consequently she charged high prices—for the risk, the expertise that would never be acknowledged and the feelings of shame she was to inspire in women afterward.

After my first trip to the Passage Cardinet, I began taking penicillin and my life was suddenly ruled by fear. I kept imagining the kitchen and the bedroom in Madame P-R's apartment, I couldn't face what would come next. I told the girls at the canteen that I was afraid because I was having a large beauty spot removed from my back. They seemed surprised that such a harmless operation should make me so nervous. Admitting I was scared gave me a huge sense of relief: for a split-second, I could see myself in a pristine operating room, attended to by a surgeon in rubber gloves, instead of an ageing nurse in some dingy back kitchen.

(To experience anew the emotions I felt back then is quite impossible. The closest I can get to the state of terror thrust upon me that week is to pick out any hostile, harsh-looking woman in her sixties waiting in line at the supermarket or the post office and to imagine that she is going to rummage around in my loins with some foreign object.)

On Wednesday January 15 I caught a train to Paris in the early afternoon. When I reached the 17th *arrondissement,* I was over an hour early for my appointment with Madame P-R. I wandered around her neighborhood. It was a wet, mild day. I entered a church, Saint-Charles-Borromée, and sat there for a long time, praying that I should not suffer. It still wasn't time. I entered a café near the Passage Cardinet and had a cup of tea while I waited. At a nearby table, some students—the only customers—were playing a game of cards, cracking jokes with the owner. I kept glancing at my watch. Just before leaving, I went downstairs to the restroom as I always did before an important event, a habit drilled into me since childhood. I stared at my reflection in the mirror above the washbasin, thinking: "I can't believe this is happening to me" and "I don't think I can take it."

Madame P-R had got everything ready. On the gas ring I noticed a saucepan of boiling water that probably contained the surgical instruments. She seemed to be in a hurry and bustled me through into the bedroom. A table covered with a white towel had been set up at the end of the bed. I stepped out of my tights and panties; I think I kept on my black skirt because it was flared. While I was undressing, she asked me, "did you bleed a lot when you lost your virginity?" She arranged the top half of my body onto a pillow on the bed and placed my hips and folded legs on the table, in a raised position. She kept talking while she was going about her business, repeating that she would insert the probe on its own. Then she told me about a housewife who had passed away on her dining-room table the week before after being injected with chloride bleach and left there by an abortionist. The story clearly angered Madame P-R, who was outraged by such manifestations of incompetence. Her words were intended to comfort me. But I wish she hadn't said them. It occurred to me later on that she was merely striving for perfection in her work.

She sat down at the foot of the bed, facing the table.

I could see her window shrouded in curtains, the windows across the street, her gray head bowed between my thighs. I had never imagined myself in this situation. I may have had a thought for the other girls, poring over their textbooks in class at that very moment, for my mother, humming her way through the ironing, or for P, strolling downtown in Bordeaux. But you don't need to picture reality to feel it around you, and knowing that life went on for most people made me wonder, "what on earth am I doing here?"

Only now can I visualize the room. It defies analysis. All I can do is sink into it. I feel that the woman who is busying herself between my legs, inserting the speculum, is giving birth to me.

At that point I killed my own mother inside me.

For many years I saw that room and those curtains the same way I had seen them from my reclining position on the bed. Now it might be a room streaming with light with Ikea furniture, belonging to a young executive who has bought the whole floor. However, I am convinced that the walls still resonate with the memory of the girls and women who went there to have a probe thrust up their belly.

There was a blinding pain. She kept saying, "stop screaming, girl" and "let me get on with my job" or maybe other words but they all meant one thing: we had to go through with it. Later I came across the same expressions in stories of women who had aborted illegally, as if the only words that mattered there and then were those conveying a sense of urgency or possibly compassion.

I can't remember how long it took her to insert the probe. I was crying. It had stopped hurting, now I just felt a weight in my stomach. She said that it was all over, that I was not to touch it. She had stuffed a large wad of cotton wool between my thighs in case the waters broke. I could walk and go to the bathroom normally. It would go away in a couple of days; if it didn't, I was to call her. We both drank coffee in the kitchen. She too was satisfied it was all over. I don't recall handing her the money.

She was concerned about my getting back home. She insisted on walking me to Pont-Cardinet station, where I could catch a train direct to Saint-Lazare. I wanted to take leave of her and be on my own. However, I didn't want to offend her by turning down her offer, prompted—little did I know at the time—by the fear that I would be found unconscious on her doorstep. She grabbed a coat but kept on her slippers.

Outdoors, everything seemed surreal. We walked side by side in the middle of the street, heading toward the far end of the Passage Cardinet, darkened by a long façade that let in only a narrow ray of light. The scene is in slow motion, daylight is fading. Nothing from my childhood or my past life could account for my being there. We passed several people; I was sure they glanced at me and could tell from the two of us what had been going on. I felt everyone had abandoned me except this elderly woman in her black overcoat who was walking beside me like my mother. Out in the street, away from her den, her gray skin repelled me. The woman who had saved me could have been a witch or an old madam.

She gave me a ticket and waited with me on the platform until the next train for Saint-Lazare drew in.

(I'm not too sure she kept on her slippers. The fact that I assumed she did, portraying her as the type of woman who would unceremoniously shuffle down to the corner store, proves that I saw her as a figure of the working-class world, from which I was gradually drifting away.)

On January 16 and 17 I waited for the contractions. I wrote to P, informing him that I never wanted to see him again, and to my parents, telling them that I wouldn't be back for the weekend—I was going to see the Viennese Waltzes. Posters advertising the event all over Rouen provided me with the perfect excuse and my parents could easily check this information in the local paper.

Nothing. I could feel no pain. On the evening of the 17th—it was a Friday—I called Madame P-R from the post office near the station. She told me to come back and see her the following morning. In my diary, which had remained blank since January 1, my entry for the 17th read: "Still nothing. Tomorrow I'm going back to see the abortionist as she hasn't succeeded."

On Saturday 18 I caught an early train to Paris. It was bitterly cold, everything was white. In the same car, two girls sitting behind me never stopped talking, punctuating their conversation with frequent bursts of laughter. Listening to them, I felt ageless.

Mme P-R greeted me with exclamations about the cold

weather and quickly ushered me inside. A man was sitting in the kitchen, a younger man with a beret. He seemed neither surprised nor embarrassed to see me there. I can't remember whether he stayed or left but he must have said something because I remember thinking he was Italian. On the table lay a basin full of steaming water with a thin red pipe floating on the surface. I realized this was the other probe she was planning to use. I hadn't seen the first one. This one reminded me of a snake. Beside the basin lay a hairbrush.

(If I had to choose one painting to symbolize that episode in my life, it would be a small table with a formica top pushed up against a wall and an enamel basin with a probe glowing on the surface. Slightly to the right—a hairbrush. I don't believe there is a single museum in the world whose collections feature a work called *The Abortionist's Studio*.)

Like before, she led me into the bedroom. This time I wasn't afraid of what she would do. It didn't hurt. As she was removing the first probe to replace it with the new one, she exclaimed, "you're in labor!" The words a midwife would use. Up to then, it hadn't occurred to me that all this could be likened to a delivery. She didn't charge extra; she simply asked me to send back the probe afterward as that particular model was difficult to find.

In the railroad car taking me back to Paris, a woman spent the whole trip meticulously filing her nails.

Madame P-R's practical contribution was over. She had done her job and had launched the mechanism that wipes out disaster. She was not paid to provide any further assistance.

(As I am writing this, I learn that a bunch of Kosovar refugees are trying to enter Britain illegally via Calais. The smugglers are charging vast sums of money and some of them disappear before the crossing. Yet nothing will stop the Kosovars or any other poverty-stricken emigrants from fleeing their native country: it's their sole means of survival. Today smugglers are vilified and pursued like abortionists were thirty years ago. No one questions the laws and world order that condone their existence. Yet surely, among those who trade in refugees, as among those who once traded in foetuses, there must be some sense of honor.

Soon afterward, I tore out the page of my address book where I had jotted down Madame P-R's name. I have never forgotten it. I came upon it six or seven years later in the guise of a sullen, fair-haired boy with rotten teeth, far too tall and too old to be in sixth grade. I couldn't call out his name to examine him or read it in an essay without associating it with the woman from the Passage Cardinet. In my mind this boy could exist only in connection with an ageing abortionist whom I imagined was his grandmother. Similarly, over the years, the man I had glimpsed in Madame P-R's kitchen, who was probably her companion, was to materialize in a small notions store on the Place Notre-Dame in Annecy—an Italian with a broad accent and a beret jammed tight on his head. So much so, that today I have trouble distinguishing the copy from the original: when I think back to the Passage Cardinet on that bitter Saturday in January, my memory slots in the man who sold me bias binding and corozo oil buttons in the Seventies, standing beside a small, nimble woman of indeterminate age.)

As soon as I reached the station, I called Doctor N. I told him that I had been fitted with a probe. Maybe I hoped he would summon me to his office, like he had done the previous month, and would take over from Madame P-R. After a long pause, he suggested that I take Masogynestril.* On hearing his voice, I understood that the last thing he wanted was to see me and that I wasn't to call him again.

(I couldn't have imagined—as I can today—that he would be sweating behind his desk, suddenly overcome with panic on hearing a young girl tell him she'd been walking around with a probe up her womb for the past three days. Faced with a terrible dilemma. If he agreed to see her, he would be forced by law to remove the device and to let the unwanted pregnancy follow its course. On the other hand, if he refused to see her, she might very well die. It was the lesser of two evils and he was on his own. So he prescribed Masogynestril.)

I walked into the nearest drugstore, just opposite the Café Metropole, to buy Doctor N's medicine. A woman asked me, "Do you have a prescription? We can't give it to you without a prescription." I was standing in the middle of the store. Two or three pharmacists in white coats stared at me from behind the counter. My failure to produce a prescription was a sure sign of guilt. I felt they could see the probe through my clothing. Rarely have I ever felt so desperate.

---

* I'm not sure of the name of this painkiller prescribed for uterine contractions, which is no longer sold in drugstores.

(Do you have a prescription? You need a prescription! I have never been able to hear these words or to see the druggist's features harden on hearing no without feeling utterly devastated.

When I write, I must guard against lyrical outbursts such as anger or pain. I would not want crying and shouting to feature in this text because they barely featured in my life at the time. Above all I wish to capture the impression of a steady flow of unhappiness, conveyed by a pharmacist's inquisitive attitude or the sight of a hairbrush by a steaming basin of water. The distress I experience on recalling certain images and on hearing certain words is beyond comparison with what I felt at the time: these are merely literary emotions; in other words they generate the act of writing and justify its veracity.)

On weekends the dorm was empty except for foreign students and a few girls whose parents lived far away. The nearby university canteen was closed. I didn't mind, I had no desire for company. Thinking back, I realize I wasn't afraid but serene: all I needed to do now was wait.

I was incapable of reading or listening to music. One

day I took a sheet of paper and drew the Passage Cardinet the way I saw it as I was leaving the abortionist's building: tall façades converging toward a crack in the background. The only time in my adult life when I have felt like drawing.

On Sunday afternoon I wandered along cold, sunlit streets in Mont-Saint-Aignan. I had grown used to the probe. It had become part of my stomach, it was an ally. My only objection—it wasn't acting fast enough.

In my diary, the entry for January 19 read: "Slight twinges of pain. I wonder how long it will take for this embryo to die and to be expelled. A bugle playing *La Marseillaise*, sounds of laughter from upstairs. That's what life is about."

(It wasn't all about unhappiness. It was something to do with the impervious need I had to picture myself once again in that room on that particular Sunday in order to write my first book—*Cleaned Out*—eight years later. The desire to cram the first twenty years of my life into that room and that Sunday.)

By Monday morning I had been walking around with a probe inside me for five days. Around midday I caught a train to Y for a brief visit to my parents, fearing that my condition on the following Saturday would not allow me to make the trip. Maybe, as was my wont, I tossed a coin to decide whether I could afford to take the risk. The weather had turned mild, my mother was airing the bedrooms. I checked my panties. They were soaking wet, blood and water oozing down the probe, which was slipping out of my vagina. I could see the small, low-roofed houses of our neighborhood with their tidy front gardens, nothing had changed since I was a kid.

(This image is gradually giving way to another one, dated nine years earlier. The large pinkish stain of blood and other bodily fluids left in the middle of my pillow by our cat, who died one afternoon in April while I was still at school and who had already been buried with her dead kittens inside her when I got back home.)

I caught the 16.20 train back to Rouen. The trip was only forty minutes long. As usual, I had stocked up with instant coffee, condensed milk and packets of cookies.

That evening the Faluche film club was showing *Battleship Potemkin*. I went there with O. Spasms of pain, which I had barely noticed at first, seared through me. Each time my stomach contracted, I held my breath and stared at the screen. The attacks became more and more frequent. By now I had lost track of the story. A huge piece of meat hanging from a hook, swarming with worms, suddenly loomed into sight. That was the last image I saw of the movie. I stood up and rushed back to the dorm. I lay down and began clinging to the bedstead in an attempt to stifle my screams. I vomited. Later on, O came into my room, the film was over. Not knowing what to do, she sat down beside me and suggested that I start breathing like a puppy, the way pregnant women are instructed to do. I could only pant between spasms and they had become continuous. It was past midnight. O went to bed, telling me to call her if I needed her. Neither of us knew what the future would hold.

I was seized with a violent urge to shit. I rushed across the corridor into the bathroom and squatted by the porcelain bowl, facing the door. I could see the tiles between my thighs. I pushed with all my strength. It burst forth like a grenade, in a spray of water that splashed the door. I saw a baby doll dangling from my loins at the end of a reddish cord. I couldn't imagine ever having had that inside me. I had to walk with it to my room. I took it in one hand—it was strangely heavy—and proceeded along the corridor, squeezing it between my thighs. I was a wild beast.

O's door was ajar, with a beam of light, I called out her name softly, "it's here."

The two of us are back in my room. I am sitting on the bed with the foetus between my legs. Neither of us knows what to do. I tell O we must cut the cord. She gets a pair of scissors; we don't know where to cut it but she goes ahead and does it. We look at the tiny body with its huge head, the eyes two blue dashes beneath translucent lids. It looks like an Indian doll. We look at the sexual organs. We seem to detect the early stages of a penis. To think I was capable of producing that. O sits down on a stool, she is crying. We are both crying in silence. It's an indescribable scene, life and death in the same breath. A sacrificial scene.

We don't know what to do with the foetus. O goes to her room to fetch an empty melba toast wrapper and I slip it inside. I walk to the bathroom with the bag. It feels like a stone inside. I turn the bag upside down above the bowl. I pull the chain.

In Japan aborted embryos are called *"mizuko"*—water babes.

The motions we went through that night came to us naturally. They seemed the only thing to do at the time.

Nothing about her bourgeois ideals or her beliefs had prepared O to sever the umbilical cord of a three-month-old foetus. Today she may have dismissed this episode as a temporary aberration, an inexplicable moment of chaos in her life. She may also hold anti-abortion views. But it was she, and she alone, who stood by my side that night, her small face crumpled with tears, acting as an improvised midwife in room 17 of the girls' dormitory.

I was losing blood. At first I didn't take any notice, I was certain everything was over. Blood was gushing from the severed cord in spurts. I lay motionless on the bed; O kept handing me towels that soaked up the blood in no time. I didn't want to deal with any doctors; up to then, I'd managed fine on my own. I tried to stand up and saw stars; I thought I was going to die of a hemorrhage. I screamed at O that I needed a doctor immediately. She went downstairs to wake up the janitor but there was no answer. Then I heard voices. I was convinced that I had already lost far too much blood.

The arrival of the doctor on night duty heralded the second part of the night. Sheer experience of life and death gave way to exposure and judgement.

He sat down on my bed and grabbed my chin: "Why did you do it? How did you do it? Answer me!" His glaring eyes bore into me. I begged him not to let me die. "Look at me! Promise me you'll never do it again! Never!" Because of his wild expression, I believed he might actually let me die if I didn't promise. He got out his prescription pad: "I'm sending you to the Hôtel-Dieu Hospital." I told him I would have preferred a clinic. He repeated the word "Hôtel-Dieu" with emphasis, implying that a hospital was the only place for a girl like me. He asked me to pay for the consultation. I was incapable of standing up so he opened the drawer of my desk and helped himself from my wallet.

(Searching through my papers, I came across a description of this scene written a few months ago. I see that I had chosen exactly the same words, "might actually let me die..." and so on. Whenever I think about my abortion in the bathroom, the same image invariably springs to mind: a bomb or a grenade erupting, the bung of a casket popping. My inability to use different words and this definitive coupling of past events with specific images barring all others, are no doubt proof that I *truly* experienced such events *in this particular manner.)*

I was taken downstairs on a stretcher. Everything was blurred, I wasn't wearing my glasses. So, the antibiotics and the self-command I had shown during the first part of the evening had been in vain; I was to end up in hospital after all. I felt that I had done all the right things up to the hemorrhage. I wondered what had gone wrong, probably our decision to cut the umbilical cord. I had lost all control.

(The same situation will probably occur after this book is published. My determination, my efforts, all this secret, and even clandestine work—no one has been apprised of the project—all this will vanish overnight. I shall have no more power over my text, exposed to the public just like my body was exposed at the Hôtel-Dieu Hospital.)

I was laid down on a rollaway bed in a hospital corridor opposite the elevator, amid a stream of people coming and going. It was never my turn to be carted away. A girl with a huge stomach turned up, accompanied by an older woman who was probably her mother. She announced that she was ready to give birth. The nurse dismissed her claims, saying it was far too early. The girl insisted on staying, an argument broke out, then the two of them left. The nurse shrugged her shoulders, "she's been having us on for the past fortnight!" I surmised she was in her early twenties, unmarried. She had kept the child yet people were no kinder to her. Girls who abort and unwed mothers from working-class Rouen were handed the same treatment. In fact, they probably despised her even more.

In the operating room, I was naked, my legs raised, my feet strapped into stirrups under a blinding light. I couldn't understand why they wanted to operate, there was nothing left in my stomach. I entreated the young surgeon to tell me what he was going to do. He stood there before my splayed thighs, shouting: "I'm no fucking plumber!" The last words I heard before succumbing to the anesthetic.

("I'm no fucking plumber!" This sentence and so many other ones that punctuated this part of my life—ordinary sentences by people who uttered them without thinking— still resonate inside my brain. I wasn't "expecting" it and nothing can deaden its impact, neither familiarity nor sociopolitical analysis. Fleetingly, I glimpse a man in a white coat with rubber gloves, beating me black and blue, yelling, "I'm no fucking plumber!" In my mind, this sentence continues to split the world in two, ramming home the distinction between, on the one hand, doctors, on the other, workers or women who abort, between those who rule and those who are ruled.)

When I woke up, it was night-time. I heard a woman come into the room and tell me for heaven's sake to be quiet. I asked her if they had taken out my ovaries. She reassured me brusquely: I had only been curetted. I was alone in a hospital room, wearing one of their gowns. I could hear babies crying. My belly was a flaccid basin.

That night I knew I had lost the body I'd had since adolescence, with its secret, living womb which had swallowed a man's penis without changing, becoming even more secret and living. Now my loins had been exposed, torn apart, my stomach scraped, opened up. A body not unlike my mother's.

I consulted the chart at the foot of the bed. Someone had written "gravid uterus." It was the first time I had seen the word "gravid;" I found it offensive. When I remembered the Latin term—*gravidus*: heavy—the meaning became clear to me. I still couldn't understand why they had written that since I was no longer pregnant. I guess they didn't want to mention my condition.

For lunch, I was given a large piece of boiled meat on some tired cabbage leaves with prominent ribs and veins, filling the whole plate. I couldn't touch it. I felt that I had been served my own placenta.

The corridor was the scene of frenzied agitation revolving around the food cart. At regular intervals, a woman's voice rang out, "custard for Madame X or Madame Y, who is breastfeeding," as if it were some kind of privilege.

The intern I had seen the night before came round. He stayed at the back of the room, looking embarrassed. I thought he was ashamed of having behaved badly toward me in the operating room. I felt sorry for him. I was wrong. The only reason why he was ashamed—I found out that night—was that he had treated a college student like an ordinary salesgirl or a factory worker because he knew nothing about me.

The lights had been out for some time. The nurse on night watch, a gray-haired woman, walked softly to the top of my bed. The glow of the night-light lent her a kindly expression. She said stiffly, "Last night, why didn't you tell the doctor you were like him?" After a moment's hesitation, I realized what she meant, in other words, "from the same world." He only discovered I was at college after the operation, probably on seeing my student union card. She mimicked the intern's reaction, a combination of anger and surprise, "why on earth didn't she tell me? why?" as though she too were outraged by my behavior. I guess I thought that she was right and that I was to blame for his aggressiveness: he had no idea who he was dealing with.

As she was leaving, she alluded to my abortion with a triumphant "you're much better off now!" The only comforting words bestowed on me while I was in hospital. I did not ascribe her remark to solidarity among women but to the assumption prevailing among "humble people" that "those in high places" enjoy the right to place themselves above the law.

(If I had been told the name of the intern who was on duty that night—January 20–21, 1964—and if I still remembered it, nothing would stop me from divulging it here. That would be a petty act of revenge indeed, and totally unfair since his attitude merely reflected a common practice in those days.)

My breasts began to swell and ache. I was told this was caused by lactation. It hadn't occurred to me that my body would start producing milk to feed a dead, three-month-old foetus. Nature pursued its inexorable course, regardless. They wrapped a long swathe around my chest, winding it round and round, pressing my breasts flat, literally pushing them into my ribcage. I feared they would never grow back into shape. A nurse's aide placed a jug of herbal tea on my bedside table: "after you've drunk all that, your breasts will stop hurting!"

When Jean T, LB and JB all came to see me together, I told them about the hemorrhage and my gruelling reception at the hospital. A light-hearted narrative which they thoroughly enjoyed and which carefully omitted the details that were to haunt me thereafter. LB and I gleefully compared our respective abortions. JB said the local grocer had told him there was no need to go all the way to Paris—a woman who lived round the corner would do it for three hundred francs. We joked about the money I could have saved, one hundred francs. Now we could afford to laugh at the fear and humiliations I had endured, and everything else that had not prevented us from transgressing.

I don't recall reading anything during the five days I spent at the Hôtel-Dieu. Transistor sets were banned. For the first time in three months, I had nothing to wait for. I lay in bed, gazing at the hospital roofs through the window.

The newborn babies would cry intermittently. Although there was no cradle in my room, I too had delivered. I felt no different from the women in the next room. In fact, I was probably wiser because of the abortion. In my student bathroom, I had given birth to both life and death. For the first time I felt caught up in a line of women, future generations would pass through us. These were gray, winter days. I floated in the midst of the world, bathed in light.

I was discharged from the hospital on Saturday, January 25. LB and JB attended to the paperwork and drove me to the station. From the nearby post office I called Doctor N and told him it was all over. He advised me to take penicillin as I had been given no medicine in hospital. I arrived at my parents' house and went straight to bed, pretending I had a cold. I asked them to call in Doctor V, the family physician. Informed of my abortion by Doctor N, he was to examine me discreetly and prescribe penicillin.

As soon as my mother was out of hearing, Doctor V began whispering excitedly, asking me who was responsible. He chuckled, "why go up to Paris? You've got old mother X only a few doors away (I had never heard of her), she knows a thing or two about it!" Now that I no longer needed them, suddenly, bevies of abortionists were springing up left, right and center. However, I had no illusions on one count: a right-wing voter and a devout churchgoer to boot, Doctor V could only impart this information now, when I no longer needed it. Sitting on my bed, he could well afford to indulge in the jocular relationship he'd always had with a bright pupil from a "humble background" who might end up in his world one day.

Of those days spent at my parents' after leaving hospital, I retain only one image. I am reclining on my bed, with the window open, reading a paperback edition of Gérard de Nerval's poems. I gaze down at my legs sheathed in black tights, basking in the sun: they are the legs of a different woman.

I returned to Rouen. It was a cold, sunny month of February. I walked back into a different world. Cars, strangers' faces, trays of food in the canteen—everything I saw was vibrant with intention. But, because of this profusion, it had all become meaningless. On the one hand, people and things were bursting with significance and, on the other, words had shed their substance. I was in a state of euphoria and acute awareness that transcended language, pursuing me even at night. I slept lightly, convinced that I was awake. A milky water babe floated before my eyes, reminding me of the dog whose corpse is plunged into ether and who persists in following a group of astronauts in a novel by Jules Verne.

I spent time at the library doing research for my thesis, which I had dropped around mid-December. Reading demanded considerable time and effort; I felt I was deciphering code. The subject of my assignment—the role of women in Surrealist writing—came across as a radiant entity, but one which could not be broken down into ideas, a dreamlike vision that could not be marshalled into a coherent argument. And yet this shapeless concept was undoubtedly real, far more real than the students hunched over their books or the fat campus policeman hovering near the girls checking references in the index. I was intoxicated, wrapped up in wordless intelligence.

I would listen to Bach's *Passion According to St John* in my room. When the Evangelist's solo voice rang out in German to celebrate the Passion of Christ, I felt the ordeal I had suffered between October and January was being recounted in an unknown language. Then came the chorus *Wohin! Wohin!* The horizons parted, the kitchen in the Passage Cardinet, the probe and the blood all became engulfed in the misery of the world and eternal death. I felt saved.

I walked along the city streets, my body harboring the secret of that night of January 20-21 as something sacred. I couldn't decide whether I had reached the outer fringes of horror or beauty. I felt proud. A feeling not unlike that experienced by lone sailors, drug addicts or thiefs, who have ventured where others fear to tread. A feeling that may partly have contributed to my writing this book.

One evening O took me to a party. I sat at the back of some-one's cellar watching other people dance, wondering at their enjoyment, evidenced by memories of Annie L's beaming face and twirling white jersey dress, all the rage that winter. I was the odd one out, attending a ritual whose meaning escaped me.

One afternoon I followed a medical student called Gérard H back to his room on the Rue Bouquet. He removed my sweater and my bra; I glanced down at my drooping, shrunken breasts, bursting with milk only two weeks before. I would have liked to tell him all about that and Madame P-R. Suddenly I felt no more desire for this boy. We ended up eating some fruitcake that his mother had baked for him.

On another afternoon I entered Saint Patrice's Church just off the Boulevard de la Marne to tell a priest that I'd had an abortion. I immediately realized this was a mistake. I felt bathed in a halo of light and for him I was a criminal. Leaving the church, I realized that I was through with religion.

A few months later, in March, at the library, I ran into Jacques S, the student who had walked me to the bus stop on my first visit to the gynecologist. He asked me how my thesis was coming along. We went out into the lobby. As usual, he kept swirling around me as he spoke. He intended to hand in his paper on Chrétien de Troyes in May and was surprised that I had only just started work. Indirectly, I intimated that I'd had an abortion. Out of pride or possibly social vindictiveness, to challenge this factory manager's son who spoke of workers as if they came from a different planet. When the truth dawned on him, he froze, staring at me with bulging eyes, mesmerized by some imaginary scene, utterly fascinated, as I remember all men were.* He kept saying, "Well done, old girl! Well done!" with a dazed expression.

I went back to see Doctor N. After giving me a thorough examination, he smiled and said proudly with a hint of approval that I had "pulled through" remarkably well. Unwittingly, he too was encouraging me to turn this painful experience into a personal victory. He gave me a contraceptive device—a diaphragm to be fitted into the back of the vagina—and two tubes of sperm jelly.

---

* I immediately identified the same feeling, powerfully expressed, in John Irving's novel *The Cider House Rules*. Through one of his characters, the author sees women who abort clandestinely die in terrible circumstances then opens a model clinic where he performs clean abortions, bringing up the children they leave behind. Entertaining fantasies of wombs and blood, he assumes the right to dispose of the life and death of women in the manner he chooses.

I didn't send the probe back to Madame P-R. I felt that, for the prices she charged, I could save myself the trouble. One day I took my parents' car, drove into the forest and threw it into some bushes. Later on, I regretted doing so.

I'm not sure how long it took me to return to normal—a term understood by all despite its vagueness—alluding to a world in which the sight of a gleaming washbasin or a row of heads on a train stops being a source of anxiety or speculation. I began working on my thesis. I took up baby-sitting in the evenings and manned the switchboard for a heart specialist to pay back the loan for the abortion. I went to the movies, saw *Charade* with Audrey Hepburn and Cary Grant, *Peau de Banane* with Jeanne Moreau and Jean-Paul Belmondo, neither of which made any impression; I had my long hair cut short and swapped my glasses for contact lenses; slipping them into place seemed as difficult and precarious as fitting the diaphragm into my vagina.

I never saw Madame P-R again. I have never stopped thinking about her. Involuntarily, this avaricious woman—whose flat was nonetheless poorly furnished—wrenched me away from my mother and into the world. She is the one to whom this book should be dedicated.

For many years I celebrated the night of January 20-21 as an anniversary.

Now I know that this ordeal and this sacrifice were necessary for me to want to have children. To accept the turmoil of reproduction inside my body and, in turn, to let the coming generations pass through me.

I have finished putting into words what I consider to be an extreme human experience, bearing on life and death, time, law, ethics and taboo—an experience that sweeps through the body.

I have rid myself of the only feeling of guilt in connection with this event: the fact that it had happened to me and I had done nothing about it. A sort of discarded present. Among all the social and psychological reasons that may account for my past, of one I am certain: these things happened to me so that I might recount them. Maybe the true purpose of my life is for my body, my sensations and my thoughts to become writing, in other words, something intelligible and universal, causing my existence to merge into the lives and heads of other people.

THIS AFTERNOON I WENT BACK to the Passage Cardinet in the 17th *arrondissement*. I had checked the route beforehand in a map of Paris. I wanted to find the café where I waited until it was time to see Madame P-R as well as the church where I sat for a long while, Saint-Charles Borromée. Only one church featured on the map—Saint-Charles-de-Monceau. It occurred to me that it might be the same one that had been renamed. I got off the Métro at Malesherbes and walked until I reached the Rue de Tocqueville. It was around four o' clock, a cold day suffused with sunlight. A new street plaque had been set up at the entrance to the Passage Cardinet. The former plaque, blackened, illegible, had been left there above the new one. The street was empty. A huge board had been erected on the ground floor of one of the buildings: "Seine-et-Oise *Département* Association of Nazi Camp Survivors and Deportees." I don't recall ever having seen it before.

I reached Madame P-R's building. I halted in front of the door; it was locked, fitted with a digital entry system. I kept on walking down the middle of the street, staring at the crack of light at the end of the alley. I passed no one and no cars went by. I felt like a puppet re-enacting a scene without the slightest hint of emotion.

At the end of the Passage Cardinet I turned right and set out in search of the church. It turned out to be Saint-Charles-de-Monceau, not Saint-Charles-Borromée. There was a statue of St Rita inside; I guess I must have lit a candle in her honor that day because she was believed to champion "lost causes." I walked back to the Rue de Tocqueville. I wondered in which café I'd had a cup of tea while I waited for my appointment with Madame P-R. From the outside, none of them looked familiar but I was sure I would recognize the downstairs bathroom where I'd been just before going to her apartment.

I went into the Café Brazza. I ordered a hot chocolate and got out some essays to mark but I couldn't read a single line. I kept telling myself that I had to check out the restroom. A young couple were kissing, leaning over the café table. Finally I stood up and asked the barman where the restroom was. He pointed to a door at the back of the café. It gave onto a tiny closet with a washbasin, a mirror just above and a second door leading to the bathroom. It was a "Turkish-style" toilet. I couldn't remember whether the café I went into thirty-five years ago had one like this. It wasn't the sort of detail I would have noticed back then, practically all public toilets were built that way: a hole in the cement with room on either side to place your feet and squat.

Standing on the platform at Malesherbes Métro station, I realized that I had gone back to the Passage Cardinet in the hope that something might happen to me.

February to October 1999

CPSIA information can be obtained
at www.ICGtesting.com
Printed in the USA
BVHW080007210522
637572BV00008B/15